Thank you very much for choosing this book.
You can also connect with me on Instagram.
Instagram URL:- https://www.instagram.com/i_mrigendrabharti.official
Thank You,
Mrigendra Bharti

Hidden Struggles; The Unseen Challenges Of Women

Mrigendra Bharti

Published by Sellbrochure Vymish Entertainment, 2024.

This is a work of fiction. Similarities to real people, places, or events are entirely coincidental.

HIDDEN STRUGGLES; THE UNSEEN CHALLENGES OF WOMEN

First edition. June 14, 2024.

Copyright © 2024 Mrigendra Bharti.

ISBN: 979-8227322456

Written by Mrigendra Bharti.

Table of Contents

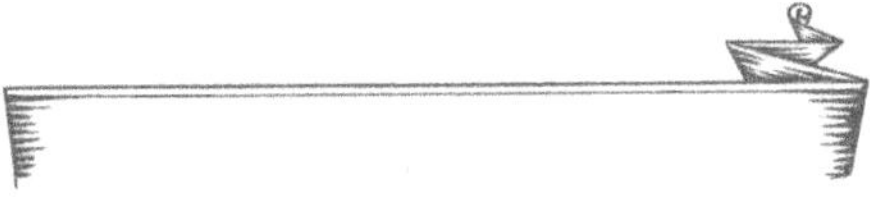

Preface

"Hidden Struggles; The Unseen Challenges Of Women" is a journey through the silent battles and unspoken dreams of women in our society. This book aims to shed light on the myriad of challenges women face, often unseen and unheard by the world around them. From societal constraints to personal battles with self-esteem and mental health, women navigate a complex web of expectations, pressures, and barriers that often go unnoticed.

Growing up, many girls are taught to dream within boundaries, to adjust and compromise rather than to break free and soar. This book delves into those boundaries, exploring the invisible chains that hold back countless women, and highlighting the strength and resilience they muster to overcome these obstacles.

Each chapter of this book is crafted to provide a comprehensive understanding of the multifaceted issues women encounter. We explore the deep-rooted societal norms that shape the lives of women, the internal and external pressures that impact their mental well-being, and the intricate dynamics of relationships that often demand more than they give.

Through real-life anecdotes, expert insights, and practical advice, "Hidden Struggles" aims to empower women to recognize their worth and potential. It calls upon society to acknowledge and support the dreams and aspirations of women, and to foster an environment where they can thrive without fear or compromise.

This book is not just for women; it is for everyone who believes in equality, justice, and the power of dreams. It is a call to action for parents, educators, leaders, and individuals to break the silence, to challenge the norms, and to create a world where every woman can rise above her struggles and achieve her true potential.

May this book inspire you to see the unseen, to hear the unheard, and to become a part of the change that allows every woman to live her life to the fullest.

Prologue

In the quiet corners of our bustling world, there exist countless stories that remain untold. These stories belong to the women who navigate life with strength and grace, yet whose struggles often go unnoticed. "Hidden Struggles; The Unseen Challenges Of Women" seeks to bring these stories to light, to uncover the silent battles fought daily by women everywhere.

Imagine a young girl named Aisha, who dreams of becoming a scientist. Each morning, she wakes up with the same passion and determination, but she is constantly reminded that her dreams are too big for someone of her gender. Her parents, although loving, encourage her to pursue a safer, more traditional path. Society tells her that her place is within the confines of her home, not in the vast, uncharted territories of science. Aisha's story is one of many that echo through the halls of households, schools, and workplaces around the world.

Then there is Leela, a bright and ambitious woman who finds herself in the throes of a high-pressure job. Every day, she juggles her professional aspirations with societal expectations of marriage and motherhood. Despite her accomplishments, she is often overlooked and underappreciated, her contributions minimized by the pervasive biases that infiltrate even the most progressive workplaces. Leela's silent frustrations and unseen sacrifices are a testament to the invisible barriers that women face in their professional lives.

And let us not forget about Sita, whose journey through mental health struggles is met with misunderstanding and stigma. Her emotional battles are dismissed as mere mood swings, and her pleas for help are often unheard. Sita's story is a poignant reminder of the importance of recognizing and addressing the mental health challenges that women endure, often in silence.

These narratives are not isolated incidents but part of a larger tapestry of experiences that define the lives of women across different cultures, backgrounds, and ages. They reveal a world where women's dreams are often constrained by societal expectations, where their contributions are undervalued, and where their mental and emotional well-being is frequently overlooked.

"Hidden Struggles; The Unseen Challenges Of Women" is a tribute to these untold stories. It is a call to recognize and honor the resilience of women who, despite the odds, continue to pursue their dreams and make a difference. Through the chapters that follow, we will explore the various facets of these struggles, offering insights and inspiration to those who read them.

This book is an invitation to see the world through the eyes of women who strive for more, to understand their journeys, and to join in the movement towards a more equitable and compassionate society. Let us embark on this journey together, to uncover the hidden struggles and to celebrate the unseen strength of women.

Acknowledgments

Writing "Hidden Struggles; The Unseen Challenges Of Women" has been a journey of immense learning and deep reflection. This book would not have been possible without the support and encouragement of many individuals, each of whom has contributed significantly to its completion.

First and foremost, I express my heartfelt gratitude to the countless women whose stories, both shared and unshared, inspired the creation of this book. Your resilience, courage, and unwavering determination are the heart and soul of this work. Thank you for being the beacons of strength that light up the path for others to follow.

I am deeply thankful to my family and friends who stood by me throughout this process. Your constant encouragement and belief in this project kept me motivated even during the most challenging times. To my parents, who instilled in me the values of empathy and justice, and to my friends who provided a listening ear and invaluable feedback, I owe you a debt of gratitude.

A special thanks to the experts and professionals who shared their insights and knowledge, enriching the content of this book. Your contributions have been invaluable in shaping a comprehensive understanding of the issues discussed herein.

To the educators and mentors who have guided me over the years, your wisdom and guidance have been instrumental in my growth as a writer and thinker. Your influence is reflected in every page of this book.

I would also like to acknowledge the supportive community of writers and researchers whose collaborative spirit and shared passion for social justice have been a source of inspiration. Your dedication to the cause of women's empowerment has been a driving force behind this work.

Finally, to every reader who picks up this book, thank you. It is your curiosity, empathy, and desire for a more equitable world that makes this journey worthwhile. I hope that "Hidden Struggles; The Unseen Challenges Of Women" resonates with you and inspires you to become an advocate for change.

This book is a collective effort, and it stands as a testament to the power of community, support, and shared dreams. Together, let us continue to uncover the hidden struggles and celebrate the unseen strength of women everywhere.

With gratitude,
Mrigendra Bharti

Introduction

In a world that is constantly evolving, the roles and expectations of women remain bound by invisible chains. Despite significant strides toward gender equality, the challenges women face are often hidden beneath the surface, masked by societal norms and unspoken biases. "Hidden Struggles; The Unseen Challenges Of Women" delves into these complexities, offering a nuanced exploration of the silent battles that shape the lives of women across various spectrums of society.

This book is not just a collection of stories; it is a mirror reflecting the realities that many women endure daily. It seeks to amplify the voices of those who are often unheard and to bring visibility to the struggles that are frequently overlooked. Through each chapter, we uncover the layers of societal expectations, familial pressures, and personal battles that women navigate as they strive to carve out their identities and pursue their dreams.

The journey begins with an examination of societal constraints—how cultural norms and stereotypes impose limitations on women's aspirations. From the confines of family expectations to the broader societal framework, we explore how these constraints manifest and impact women's lives. The narrative then transitions into the realm of self-esteem and support, highlighting the crucial role of encouragement and validation in empowering women to break free from these invisible barriers.

Mental health emerges as a pivotal theme, addressing the emotional and psychological challenges women face. Mood swings, stress, and the often-misunderstood landscape of women's mental health are discussed with empathy and insight, underscoring the need for greater awareness and support systems. Relationships and compromises further reveal the intricate dynamics women must navigate, whether within their families, romantic partnerships, or societal roles.

Ultimately, this book is a call to action. It is an invitation to see the world through the eyes of women who strive, often against overwhelming odds, to achieve their goals. By understanding their journeys, we can begin to challenge and change the societal structures that perpetuate these struggles. Each chapter concludes with practical advice and inspirational stories, offering a roadmap for both women seeking to overcome their challenges and allies who wish to support them.

"Hidden Struggles; The Unseen Challenges Of Women" is a tribute to the resilience and strength of women everywhere. It is a testament to their unwavering spirit and an acknowledgment of the silent battles they fight. Through this book, I hope to inspire readers to listen, understand, and advocate for a world where every woman's potential is recognized and nurtured.

Join me on this journey to uncover the hidden struggles and celebrate the unseen strength of women. Together, let us work towards a future where equality is not just an ideal but a lived reality for all.

Chapter 1: Societal Constraints

Part 1: Family Boundaries

From the moment a girl is born, she is enveloped in a web of familial expectations and societal norms that dictate her every move. Within the confines of her family, she learns the subtle art of obedience and the unspoken rules of conformity. Her dreams, her aspirations, her very identity are shaped by the roles assigned to her based on her gender.

At an early age, girls are taught the importance of being docile and accommodating, of putting the needs of others before their own. They are encouraged to excel in domestic duties, to master the art of homemaking, and to prioritize the well-being of their families above all else. These lessons are ingrained in their minds from childhood, reinforced by the words and actions of their parents and elders.

For many girls, the family becomes both a sanctuary and a prison—a place of love and warmth, but also one of stifling expectations and suffocating traditions. They learn to navigate the delicate balance between filial duty and personal ambition, often sacrificing the latter in favor of the former. Their dreams are put on hold, their aspirations deferred, as they dedicate themselves to fulfilling the roles assigned to them by society.

The pressure to conform to these familial expectations can be overwhelming. Girls are constantly reminded of the consequences of stepping out of line, of straying from the path laid out for them by tradition and custom. They learn to suppress their desires, to silence their voices, to shrink themselves to fit into the narrow confines of acceptability.

Yet, amidst the sea of expectations that threaten to engulf them, some girls dare to dream. They harbor secret aspirations, hidden desires, burning passions that refuse to be extinguished. They yearn for more—for freedom, for autonomy, for a life of their own choosing. But breaking free from the shackles of familial expectations is no easy feat. It requires courage, determination, and a willingness to defy the norms that have governed their lives for generations.

In the quiet moments of solitude, away from the prying eyes of their families, these girls dare to imagine a different future for themselves. They dream of pursuing higher education, of embarking on careers that fulfill them, of charting their own course in life. But these dreams are fragile, delicate, easily shattered by the weight of societal judgment and familial disapproval.

For every girl who dares to dream, there are countless others who remain trapped in the cycle of expectation and obligation. They resign themselves to a fate dictated by others, sacrificing their own happiness and fulfillment in the process. Their voices go unheard, their dreams unfulfilled, as they continue to toil in the shadows of those who came before them.

The story of familial expectations is a complex one, fraught with tension, contradiction, and unspoken longing. It is a story of love and sacrifice, of duty and obligation, of tradition and change. And for many girls, it is a story that unfolds silently, invisibly, as they navigate the intricate dance between the desires of their hearts and the expectations of their families.

Part 2: Societal Norms

Beyond the boundaries of the family unit, girls encounter a broader landscape of societal norms and expectations that shape their identities and dictate their choices. From the moment they step outside their homes, they are confronted with a myriad of unwritten rules and invisible barriers that govern their behavior and limit their potential.

In schools, classrooms become microcosms of society, where gender roles are reinforced and expectations are subtly communicated through the curriculum, classroom dynamics, and interactions with peers and teachers. Girls are encouraged to excel in certain subjects—typically those perceived as feminine—such as language arts and social sciences, while boys dominate fields like mathematics and science. These subtle messages, though often unintentional, reinforce stereotypes and perpetuate inequalities from a young age.

As girls transition into adolescence, societal expectations become even more pronounced. They are bombarded with messages from the media, popular culture, and social circles that dictate how they should look, dress, and behave. They are taught to prioritize physical appearance over intellect, to seek validation from others rather than from within. The pressure to conform to these unrealistic standards of beauty and femininity can be overwhelming, leading to low self-esteem, body image issues, and a sense of inadequacy.

Moreover, societal norms dictate the acceptable roles and behaviors of women in various spheres of life. In the workplace, women often encounter the glass ceiling—a barrier that prevents them from advancing to higher positions of leadership and authority. They are subjected to microaggressions, discrimination, and harassment, which undermine their confidence and hinder their professional growth. Despite their qualifications and capabilities, women continue to face barriers to entry and advancement in male-dominated industries and professions.

In the realm of relationships, societal norms dictate the acceptable roles and behaviors of women in romantic partnerships. They are expected to be nurturing, supportive, and submissive, while men are encouraged to be assertive, dominant, and in control. These gendered expectations perpetuate power imbalances and reinforce unhealthy dynamics within relationships, leading to feelings of resentment, inadequacy, and disempowerment.

At every turn, girls and women are confronted with societal norms and expectations that seek to define and confine them. Whether it is in the classroom, the workplace, or the home, they are reminded of their place in society and the limitations imposed upon them by their gender. Yet, despite these challenges, many women refuse to be constrained by societal expectations. They challenge the status quo, defy stereotypes, and carve out their own paths in life, inspiring others to do the same.

The story of societal norms is a complex one, shaped by centuries of tradition, culture, and history. It is a story of power and privilege, of oppression and resistance, of conformity and rebellion. And for many girls and women, it is a story that unfolds silently, invisibly, as they navigate the intricate web of expectations that surrounds them.

Part 3: Cultural Pressures

Within the tapestry of societal constraints, cultural pressures weave a complex pattern that further restricts the freedoms and aspirations of girls and women. Cultural norms, traditions, and expectations dictate every aspect of their lives, from the way they dress to the roles they play within their communities.

In many cultures, girls are raised with the understanding that their primary purpose is to uphold the honor and reputation of their families. They are taught to be modest, obedient, and deferential, traits that are prized above all others. Any deviation from these expectations is seen as a threat to the fabric of society, inviting shame and ostracism upon themselves and their families.

One of the most pervasive cultural pressures faced by girls and women is the expectation of marriage and motherhood. From a young age, they are groomed for these roles, taught to prioritize the needs of their future husbands and children above their own. Marriage is often seen as the ultimate achievement, the culmination of a girl's worth and value in society. Those who remain unmarried or choose to delay marriage are viewed with suspicion and pity, deemed incomplete or undesirable by their communities.

Moreover, cultural norms dictate the acceptable expression of femininity and womanhood, often imposing rigid standards of behavior and appearance. Girls are expected to conform to these standards from a young age, suppressing their natural inclinations and desires in favor of societal approval. They learn to perform femininity, to embody the idealized image of the "perfect woman" as defined by their culture, even if it means sacrificing their authenticity and individuality in the process.

The pressure to conform to cultural expectations can be suffocating, leading many girls and women to internalize feelings of shame, guilt, and inadequacy. They are constantly reminded of their perceived shortcomings, their failures to meet the unrealistic standards set by their communities. This internalized oppression manifests in various ways, from self-doubt and low self-esteem to anxiety and depression, robbing them of their sense of agency and self-worth.

Furthermore, cultural pressures extend beyond the individual to the collective, shaping the attitudes and behaviors of entire communities. In many cultures, women are marginalized and excluded from positions of power and influence, relegated to subordinate roles within the social hierarchy. Their voices are silenced, their contributions overlooked, as they struggle to assert their rights and claim their rightful place in society.

Yet, despite the overwhelming pressures they face, many girls and women find ways to resist and defy cultural expectations. They challenge the status quo, question traditional norms, and assert their rights to autonomy and self-determination. Through acts of courage and defiance, they pave the way for future generations of women to follow, inspiring hope and instilling a sense of possibility in the hearts of those who dare to dream of a different future.

The story of cultural pressures is a complex one, shaped by centuries of tradition, belief, and heritage. It is a story of resilience and resistance, of struggle and triumph, of oppression and liberation. And for many girls and women, it is a story that unfolds silently, invisibly, as they navigate the intricate maze of cultural expectations that surround them.

Part 4: Economic Realities

In addition to familial, societal, and cultural pressures, girls and women also grapple with the harsh realities of economic inequality and financial insecurity. Economic constraints further restrict their choices and opportunities, perpetuating cycles of poverty and marginalization that disproportionately affect women.

From a young age, girls are confronted with the stark realities of economic disparity. They witness firsthand the struggles of their families to make ends meet, to put food on the table, to afford basic necessities. They learn to navigate the complexities of financial insecurity, often sacrificing their own needs and desires in order to alleviate the burden on their families.

For many girls, access to education is limited by economic factors. They may be forced to drop out of school to help support their families financially, foregoing their dreams of a brighter future in favor of immediate economic survival. Even those who are able to attend school often face barriers such as lack of resources, inadequate infrastructure, and gender-based discrimination, further perpetuating the cycle of poverty and inequality.

Moreover, economic constraints impact women's ability to access healthcare, reproductive services, and other essential resources. They may be unable to afford medical treatment or preventive care, leading to poor health outcomes and increased vulnerability to disease. Economic insecurity also limits their ability to make choices about their own bodies and reproductive health, perpetuating cycles of gender-based violence and reproductive coercion.

In the workforce, women face systemic barriers to entry and advancement, including wage discrimination, occupational segregation, and lack of access to opportunities for skill development and career advancement. They are often relegated to low-paying, precarious jobs with few benefits and little opportunity for upward mobility. The gender pay gap further exacerbates economic inequality, leaving women financially vulnerable and dependent on others for their economic well-being.

As a result of these economic realities, many girls and women are forced to make difficult choices about their futures. They may be compelled to marry early, enter into exploitative labor arrangements, or engage in risky behaviors in order to survive. Economic insecurity leaves them vulnerable to exploitation, abuse, and exploitation, perpetuating cycles of poverty and inequality that are difficult to break.

Yet, despite the formidable obstacles they face, many girls and women demonstrate remarkable resilience and resourcefulness in the face of economic adversity. They find creative ways to support themselves and their families, to pursue their dreams and aspirations, despite the odds stacked against them. Through entrepreneurship, education, and community organizing, they challenge the structures of economic inequality and advocate for a more just and equitable society.

The story of economic realities is a sobering one, shaped by systemic inequalities and entrenched power dynamics. It is a story of struggle and survival, of resilience and resistance, of oppression and liberation. And for many girls and women, it is a story that unfolds silently, invisibly, as they navigate the harsh realities of economic inequality and strive to build a better future for themselves and their communities.

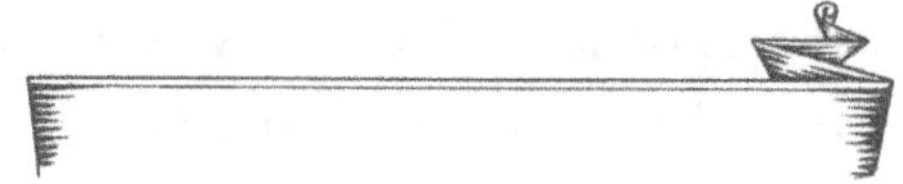

Chapter 2: Gendered Expectations in Education

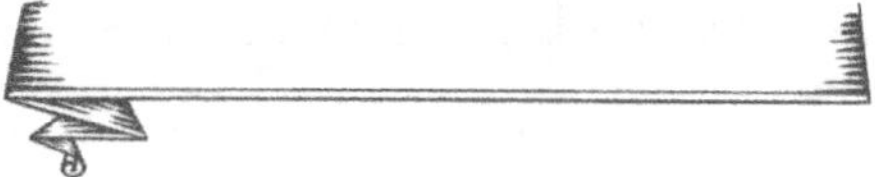

Part 1: Access and Opportunity

In the realm of education, girls and women face a myriad of challenges that stem from deeply ingrained gendered expectations and systemic inequalities. Despite progress in recent decades, disparities persist in access to education, quality of schooling, and opportunities for academic and professional advancement.

At the most fundamental level, access to education remains a barrier for many girls around the world. Cultural norms, economic constraints, and gender biases often conspire to deny girls the opportunity to attend school. In some communities, girls are seen as less deserving of an education than boys, leading to disparities in enrollment rates and dropout rates. Moreover, girls may face additional barriers such as distance to school, lack of transportation, and safety concerns, which further limit their access to educational opportunities.

Even for those girls who are able to attend school, the quality of education they receive may be subpar compared to that of their male counterparts. Gender biases may manifest in curriculum materials, teaching methods, and classroom interactions, perpetuating stereotypes and limiting girls' academic potential. Moreover, girls may be discouraged from pursuing certain fields of study or extracurricular activities deemed more appropriate for boys, further narrowing their educational horizons.

As girls progress through the education system, they encounter additional challenges related to academic and professional advancement. Stereotypes about girls' abilities in certain subjects, such as mathematics and science, may discourage them from pursuing careers in STEM fields. Moreover, girls may face barriers to accessing advanced coursework, mentorship opportunities, and extracurricular activities that are essential for academic and professional success.

Gender biases also play a role in shaping girls' aspirations and career choices. From a young age, girls are socialized to prioritize caregiving roles and traditionally feminine professions, such as teaching, nursing, and social work. They may lack exposure to role models and mentors in non-traditional fields, leading to a lack of confidence and self-efficacy in pursuing careers outside of their perceived gender roles.

Furthermore, girls and women often face systemic barriers to entry and advancement in higher education and the workforce. They may encounter discrimination and harassment in academic and professional settings, as well as unequal access to resources and opportunities for career advancement. The gender pay gap and lack of representation in leadership positions further perpetuate inequalities, limiting girls' and women's ability to achieve their full potential.

Despite these challenges, girls and women around the world continue to defy expectations and strive for excellence in their educational and professional pursuits. They challenge stereotypes, break down barriers, and advocate for gender equality in education and beyond. Through their resilience and determination, they inspire future generations of girls to pursue their dreams and aspirations, regardless of the obstacles they may face.

In conclusion, gendered expectations in education continue to pose significant challenges for girls and women worldwide. Addressing these challenges requires a multi-faceted approach that addresses systemic inequalities, challenges gender stereotypes, and promotes equal access to educational opportunities for all. By empowering girls and women to pursue their educational and professional aspirations, we can create a more just and equitable world for future generations.

Part 2: Stereotypes and Bias

Within the educational system, girls and women encounter pervasive stereotypes and biases that shape their experiences and opportunities. These stereotypes reinforce traditional gender roles and limit girls' and women's aspirations, perpetuating inequality and hindering their academic and professional advancement.

One of the most prevalent stereotypes faced by girls in education is the belief that certain subjects are "masculine" or "feminine" in nature. Mathematics and science, for example, are often perceived as male-dominated fields, while language arts and humanities are seen as more suitable for girls. These stereotypes not only influence girls' academic choices but also contribute to the underrepresentation of women in STEM (Science, Technology, Engineering, and Mathematics) fields, where they face barriers to entry and advancement.

Moreover, girls may encounter biases in the classroom that affect their academic performance and self-confidence. Teachers may unwittingly reinforce gender stereotypes through subtle cues and interactions, such as praising boys for their intelligence and girls for their effort. These biases can have a profound impact on girls' self-esteem and motivation, leading them to doubt their abilities and disengage from academic pursuits.

Outside the classroom, girls are bombarded with messages from society and the media that reinforce narrow stereotypes of femininity and masculinity. They are pressured to conform to unrealistic beauty standards and traditional gender roles, which can distract them from their academic goals and limit their potential. Moreover, girls who deviate from these stereotypes may face bullying and social ostracism, further reinforcing the pressure to conform.

In addition to stereotypes and biases, girls and women may also face discrimination and harassment in educational settings. They may be subjected to sexist remarks, sexual harassment, and gender-based violence, which can create hostile learning environments and undermine their sense of safety and well-being. Moreover, girls from marginalized communities, such as those from low-income families or ethnic minorities, may face intersecting forms of discrimination that further compound their challenges in accessing quality education.

Despite these obstacles, many girls and women demonstrate remarkable resilience and determination in the face of adversity. They challenge stereotypes, defy expectations, and advocate for gender equality in education, inspiring others to do the same. Through initiatives such as Girls' Education and empowerment programs, they seek to dismantle the barriers that limit girls' and women's access to education and create a more inclusive and equitable learning environment for all.

In conclusion, addressing stereotypes and biases in education is essential for promoting gender equality and empowering girls and women to fulfill their potential. By challenging traditional gender norms, fostering inclusive learning environments, and promoting diversity and representation in education, we can create a world where every girl has the opportunity to thrive and succeed, regardless of her gender.

Part 3: Cultural and Societal Barriers

In addition to stereotypes and biases, girls and women face cultural and societal barriers that impede their access to education and limit their opportunities for academic and professional advancement. These barriers are deeply rooted in patriarchal structures and traditional norms that prioritize the education of boys over girls and perpetuate gender inequality.

One of the most pervasive cultural barriers to girls' education is the belief that their primary role is to fulfill domestic duties and caregiving responsibilities within the family. In many societies, girls are expected to prioritize marriage and motherhood over academic pursuits, leading to early dropout rates and limited access to educational opportunities. Moreover, cultural practices such as child marriage and female genital mutilation further exacerbate the challenges faced by girls in accessing education, perpetuating cycles of poverty and inequality.

Societal expectations regarding gender roles also play a significant role in shaping girls' educational experiences. Girls may be discouraged from pursuing higher education or non-traditional career paths, as these are seen as threatening to traditional notions of masculinity and femininity. Moreover, girls may face pressure to conform to societal expectations of modesty and obedience, which can limit their freedom to express themselves and pursue their interests.

Furthermore, girls from marginalized communities face intersecting forms of discrimination and exclusion that further compound their challenges in accessing education. Girls from ethnic minorities, indigenous backgrounds, or low-income families may face additional barriers such as language barriers, lack of access to resources, and systemic discrimination in educational systems. These structural inequalities perpetuate cycles of poverty and marginalization, leaving girls and women trapped in intergenerational cycles of disadvantage.

Despite these challenges, grassroots movements and advocacy efforts are working to dismantle cultural and societal barriers to girls' education. Organizations and activists around the world are advocating for policy changes, community outreach programs, and awareness campaigns to promote gender equality in education and empower girls to fulfill their potential. Through initiatives such as scholarships, mentorship programs, and vocational training, they seek to provide girls with the support and resources they need to overcome barriers and succeed in school and beyond.

In conclusion, addressing cultural and societal barriers to girls' education is essential for promoting gender equality and empowering girls and women to reach their full potential. By challenging traditional norms, advocating for policy changes, and investing in girls' education, we can create a more inclusive and equitable world where every girl has the opportunity to thrive and succeed, regardless of her gender or background.

Part 4: Systemic Inequalities

Systemic inequalities within educational systems perpetuate gendered expectations and limit the opportunities available to girls and women. These inequalities are embedded in policies, practices, and institutional structures that prioritize the needs and interests of boys and perpetuate gender bias and discrimination.

One of the most glaring examples of systemic inequality in education is the disparity in funding and resources allocated to girls' schools compared to boys' schools. In many communities, girls' schools are underfunded, understaffed, and lack basic infrastructure such as classrooms, textbooks, and sanitation facilities. This lack of investment in girls' education perpetuates gender disparities in academic achievement and limits girls' opportunities for advancement.

Moreover, educational policies and practices often reinforce gender stereotypes and biases, further perpetuating inequality. Standardized testing and curriculum materials may contain gendered language and examples that reinforce traditional gender roles and limit girls' aspirations. Teachers may also hold unconscious biases that affect their interactions with students, leading to differential treatment and opportunities based on gender.

In addition to disparities in resources and opportunities, girls and women also face systemic barriers to entry and advancement in higher education and the workforce. Admission criteria may be biased against girls, favoring boys' performance in certain subjects or extracurricular activities. Furthermore, girls may face discrimination and harassment in academic and professional settings, hindering their ability to succeed and thrive.

Another systemic barrier to girls' education is the lack of representation and role models in educational leadership positions. Women are underrepresented in decision-making roles such as school boards, university administrations, and government ministries of education. This lack of representation perpetuates gender biases and limits girls' access to opportunities for mentorship and support.

Despite these challenges, there is growing recognition of the need to address systemic inequalities in education and empower girls and women to reach their full potential. Initiatives such as gender-responsive education policies, teacher training programs, and affirmative action measures are being implemented to promote gender equality in education and ensure that girls have equal access to opportunities for learning and advancement.

In conclusion, addressing systemic inequalities in education is essential for promoting gender equality and empowering girls and women to realize their rights and potential. By challenging gender stereotypes, advocating for policy changes, and investing in girls' education, we can create a more inclusive and equitable world where every girl has the opportunity to thrive and succeed, regardless of her gender or background.

Part 5: Overcoming Challenges

Despite the myriad challenges and barriers faced by girls and women in education, there are numerous examples of resilience, innovation, and progress that offer hope for a more equitable future. Across the globe, individuals and organizations are working tirelessly to address gender disparities in education and empower girls and women to reach their full potential.

One of the most effective strategies for overcoming challenges in girls' education is community engagement and empowerment. By involving local communities in decision-making processes and raising awareness about the importance of girls' education, grassroots organizations are able to mobilize support and resources to improve access to schooling for girls. Initiatives such as parent-teacher associations, community-led literacy programs, and girls' education committees are making a tangible difference in the lives of girls and women, empowering them to claim their right to education.

Furthermore, advocacy efforts at the national and international levels have led to significant progress in advancing girls' education and promoting gender equality in schools. Organizations such as UNESCO, UNICEF, and the Malala Fund are working to raise awareness about the importance of girls' education, advocate for policy changes, and mobilize resources to support girls' schooling. Through initiatives such as the Global Partnership for Education and the Education Cannot Wait fund, these organizations are working to ensure that every girl has the opportunity to receive a quality education, regardless of her circumstances.

In addition to advocacy and community engagement, innovations in technology and education are also playing a crucial role in expanding access to schooling for girls. Mobile learning platforms, distance education programs, and digital literacy initiatives are providing girls with opportunities to learn outside the traditional classroom setting, overcoming barriers such as distance, cost, and cultural norms. Moreover, initiatives such as girls' coding camps, STEM education programs, and vocational training opportunities are equipping girls with the skills and knowledge they need to thrive in the 21st-century economy.

Finally, investing in girls' education is not only a matter of social justice but also a sound economic decision. Studies have shown that educating girls not only improves their individual livelihoods but also has far-reaching benefits for their families, communities, and societies as a whole. Girls who receive an education are more likely to marry later, have fewer children, and contribute to household income, leading to improvements in health, economic development, and social cohesion.

In conclusion, while the challenges facing girls and women in education are significant, they are not insurmountable. Through concerted efforts to address systemic inequalities, empower communities, and invest in innovative solutions, we can create a future where every girl has the opportunity to fulfill her potential and contribute to a more just and equitable world.

Chapter 3: Self-Esteem and Support

Part 1: Lack of Self-Confidence

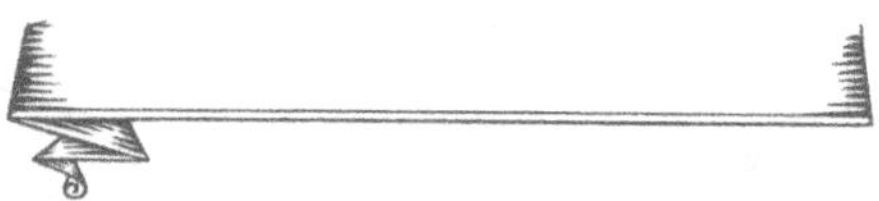

In the intricate tapestry of societal expectations and gendered norms, the journey of self-esteem for women begins with the delicate thread of self-confidence. From a tender age, girls are often confronted with subtle cues and overt messages that undermine their belief in their abilities and worth. These messages, woven into the fabric of everyday life, shape the contours of their self-image and influence the trajectory of their aspirations.

The lack of self-confidence among girls can be traced back to a myriad of factors, including societal stereotypes, familial expectations, and personal experiences. From an early age, girls are bombarded with messages that suggest their worth is contingent upon their appearance, behavior, and conformity to traditional gender roles. These messages seep into their subconscious, planting seeds of doubt and insecurity that can persist well into adulthood.

Moreover, societal norms often dictate narrow definitions of success and worth that are difficult for girls to attain. From academic achievement to physical appearance, girls are held to impossibly high standards that leave little room for imperfection or deviation. The pressure to excel in all areas of life can be overwhelming, leading to feelings of inadequacy and self-doubt.

In addition to external pressures, girls may also face internal barriers to self-confidence, such as imposter syndrome and perfectionism. They may doubt their abilities and accomplishments, attributing their success to luck or external factors rather than their own skills and efforts. This self-doubt can prevent girls from taking risks, pursuing their passions, and advocating for themselves in academic and professional settings.

Furthermore, the lack of representation and visibility of successful women in various fields can also contribute to feelings of self-doubt and inadequacy among girls. Without role models and mentors to look up to, girls may struggle to envision themselves in leadership positions or non-traditional careers, limiting their aspirations and potential.

Despite these challenges, there are strategies and interventions that can help girls build self-confidence and overcome self-doubt. Encouraging girls to pursue their interests, take on challenges, and celebrate their achievements can help boost their self-esteem and resilience. Providing positive reinforcement, constructive feedback, and mentorship opportunities can also empower girls to recognize their strengths and value their unique contributions.

Moreover, creating inclusive and supportive environments in schools, families, and communities can help counteract the negative messages and stereotypes that undermine girls' confidence. By promoting gender equality, challenging traditional gender roles, and fostering a culture of respect and empowerment, we can create a world where every girl feels valued, capable, and worthy of success.

In conclusion, addressing the lack of self-confidence among girls is essential for promoting gender equality and empowering girls to reach their full potential. By challenging societal norms, providing support and mentorship, and creating inclusive environments, we can help girls recognize their inherent worth and believe in their ability to shape their own destinies.

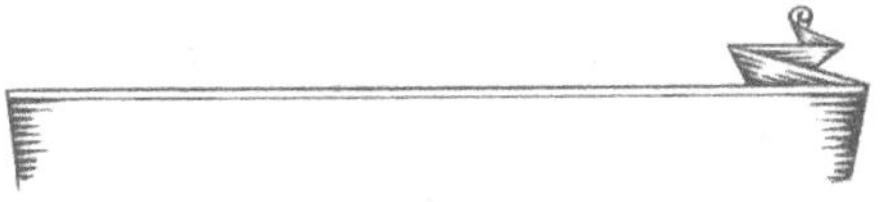

Part 2: Lack of Support

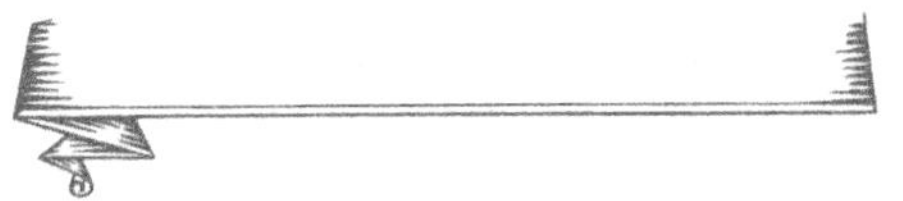

In the labyrinth of self-discovery, support serves as a guiding light, illuminating the path toward self-actualization and empowerment. However, for many girls, the journey is fraught with obstacles, as they navigate a landscape devoid of the support and encouragement they need to thrive.

The lack of support can manifest in various forms, from familial disapproval to societal indifference. In many communities, girls are discouraged from pursuing their dreams and aspirations, relegated to the sidelines while their male counterparts are given preferential treatment and opportunities for success. This disparity in support sends a clear message to girls: their dreams are not worth pursuing, their voices are not worth hearing, and their worth is contingent upon their ability to conform to societal expectations.

Moreover, girls may also face resistance and skepticism from within their own families, as they challenge traditional gender roles and expectations. Parents and relatives may discourage girls from pursuing non-traditional careers or higher education, fearing that they will deviate from the prescribed path of marriage and motherhood. This lack of familial support can be devastating for girls, eroding their confidence and self-esteem and leaving them feeling isolated and alone in their aspirations.

Furthermore, girls may also encounter barriers to support in educational and professional settings, where gender biases and discrimination can undermine their confidence and opportunities for success. Teachers may overlook girls' achievements and contributions, favoring their male peers or perpetuating stereotypes about girls' abilities and interests. Similarly, in the workplace, women may face unequal treatment and opportunities for advancement, as they navigate a male-dominated environment that prioritizes masculine traits and behaviors.

The absence of support can have profound consequences for girls' mental health and well-being, leading to feelings of isolation, self-doubt, and depression. Without the encouragement and validation they need to thrive, girls may struggle to assert themselves, advocate for their needs, and pursue their passions. This lack of support perpetuates a cycle of disempowerment and dependency, as girls are denied the resources and opportunities they need to fulfill their potential.

Despite these challenges, there are avenues for support and empowerment available to girls, if only they are given the opportunity to access them. Programs and initiatives aimed at promoting girls' education, leadership, and self-esteem can provide girls with the tools and resources they need to succeed. Mentorship programs, peer support groups, and community-based organizations can also offer girls the guidance and encouragement they need to navigate the challenges they face and pursue their dreams with confidence and determination.

In conclusion, addressing the lack of support for girls is essential for promoting gender equality and empowering girls to reach their full potential. By challenging societal norms, providing support and mentorship, and creating inclusive environments, we can help girls recognize their inherent worth and believe in their ability to shape their own destinies.

Part 3: Friends and Allies

In the intricate dance of self-discovery, friends and allies serve as steadfast companions, offering support, encouragement, and a shoulder to lean on during times of uncertainty and doubt. For many girls, friendships play a crucial role in shaping their self-esteem and sense of belonging, providing a safe space to explore their identities, express their thoughts and feelings, and seek guidance and support from those who understand and accept them unconditionally.

Friendships offer girls a sense of camaraderie and connection that is often lacking in other areas of their lives. Through shared experiences and mutual support, girls are able to cultivate meaningful relationships that bolster their confidence, resilience, and sense of self-worth. Whether through laughter and camaraderie or through shared struggles and triumphs, friendships provide girls with a sense of belonging and acceptance that is essential for their emotional well-being and personal growth.

Moreover, friendships can also serve as a source of inspiration and empowerment, as girls witness the strength, courage, and resilience of their peers. Seeing other girls pursue their passions, overcome obstacles, and assert themselves in the face of adversity can instill a sense of confidence and determination in girls, motivating them to pursue their own dreams and aspirations with conviction and resolve.

In addition to friendships, girls may also find support and allies in other important figures in their lives, such as teachers, mentors, and community leaders. These individuals can serve as role models and mentors, offering guidance, encouragement, and practical advice to help girls navigate the challenges they face and pursue their goals with confidence and determination.

Furthermore, the power of collective action and solidarity cannot be overstated in the quest for empowerment and equality. By coming together as a community, girls can amplify their voices, advocate for their rights, and effect meaningful change in their schools, communities, and beyond. Through collective action and solidarity, girls can challenge stereotypes, dismantle barriers, and create a more inclusive and equitable world where every girl has the opportunity to thrive and succeed.

In conclusion, friendships and allies play a crucial role in shaping girls' self-esteem and sense of empowerment. By cultivating supportive relationships, seeking guidance and encouragement from those who understand and accept them, and coming together as a community to advocate for their rights, girls can overcome the challenges they face and pursue their dreams with confidence and determination.

Part 4: Building Self-Confidence

In the intricate tapestry of self-discovery, self-confidence stands as the cornerstone upon which girls build their dreams and aspirations. Yet, for many, the journey toward self-assurance is fraught with obstacles and challenges that threaten to undermine their sense of worth and potential. In this final part of Chapter 2, we explore strategies and techniques to help girls cultivate self-confidence and assert themselves in a world that often seeks to diminish their voices and aspirations.

One of the most powerful tools for building self-confidence is the practice of self-affirmation and positive self-talk. By consciously acknowledging their strengths, accomplishments, and unique qualities, girls can counteract the negative messages and self-doubt that may arise from societal expectations and stereotypes. Through daily affirmations and reflections, girls can reaffirm their worth and value, empowering themselves to pursue their goals with courage and conviction.

Moreover, setting achievable goals and celebrating small victories along the way can help girls build confidence and resilience in the face of adversity. By breaking down larger aspirations into manageable steps and recognizing their progress and achievements, girls can build momentum and confidence in their ability to overcome challenges and succeed in their endeavors.

Additionally, seeking out opportunities for growth and learning can help girls expand their comfort zones and develop new skills and competencies. Whether through academic pursuits, extracurricular activities, or volunteer work, girls can challenge themselves to step outside of their comfort zones, take risks, and embrace new experiences that foster personal growth and development.

Furthermore, surrounding themselves with supportive and empowering individuals can provide girls with the encouragement and validation they need to believe in themselves and their abilities. Whether through friendships, mentorship relationships, or participation in supportive communities and organizations, girls can find strength and inspiration in the company of those who believe in their potential and champion their aspirations.

Finally, practicing self-care and prioritizing their well-being is essential for maintaining confidence and resilience in the face of life's challenges. By taking time to nurture their physical, emotional, and mental health, girls can recharge their spirits, replenish their energy, and cultivate a sense of inner peace and balance that serves as a foundation for self-confidence and self-assurance.

In conclusion, building self-confidence is a journey of self-discovery and empowerment that requires courage, resilience, and determination. By practicing self-affirmation, setting achievable goals, seeking out opportunities for growth, surrounding themselves with supportive individuals, and prioritizing self-care, girls can cultivate the confidence and self-assurance they need to pursue their dreams and aspirations with courage and conviction.

Chapter 4: Mental Health and Mood Swings

Part 1: Emotional Turbulence

In the labyrinth of adolescence and womanhood, emotions swirl like a tempest, shaping the landscape of girls' lives in profound and often unpredictable ways. From the exhilarating highs of joy and excitement to the crushing depths of sadness and despair, girls experience a rollercoaster of emotions that can leave them feeling overwhelmed, confused, and alone in their struggles.

At the heart of this emotional turbulence lie the complex interplay of hormonal changes, societal pressures, and personal experiences that shape girls' emotional landscapes. As girls navigate the transition from childhood to adulthood, they are confronted with a whirlwind of emotions that can be difficult to understand and manage. From the hormonal fluctuations of puberty to the societal expectations of femininity and womanhood, girls are bombarded with messages and influences that shape their emotional experiences and perceptions of themselves.

Moreover, girls may also face unique challenges and stressors that contribute to their emotional turbulence. From academic pressures and social expectations to family dynamics and personal relationships, girls must navigate a myriad of stressors and responsibilities that can take a toll on their mental health and well-being. The pressure to excel in school, conform to societal norms, and meet familial expectations can leave girls feeling overwhelmed, anxious, and depressed.

Furthermore, girls may also grapple with issues related to self-esteem, body image, and identity that can exacerbate their emotional struggles. In a society that places a premium on physical appearance and perfection, girls may internalize unrealistic beauty standards and compare themselves unfavorably to their peers, leading to feelings of inadequacy and low self-worth. Similarly, questions of identity and belonging can arise as girls navigate the complexities of adolescence and explore their evolving sense of self.

In addition to these internal challenges, girls may also face external barriers to seeking help and support for their emotional struggles. Stigma surrounding mental health issues, lack of access to resources and support services, and cultural taboos around seeking help can all contribute to girls' reluctance to reach out for assistance when they need it most. As a result, many girls suffer in silence, grappling with their emotions alone and without the support they need to heal and thrive.

Despite these challenges, there is hope for girls struggling with emotional turbulence. By destigmatizing mental health issues, promoting open and honest conversations about emotions, and providing access to support services and resources, we can create a culture of support and empowerment that encourages girls to seek help when they need it. Through education, advocacy, and community outreach, we can ensure that every girl has the opportunity to access the care and support she needs to navigate life's challenges with resilience and strength.

Part 2: Frustration and Stress

In the tumultuous journey of adolescence and womanhood, girls often find themselves grappling with the weight of frustration and stress, as they navigate the complexities of school, relationships, and personal growth. From academic pressures and social expectations to familial responsibilities and personal aspirations, girls are confronted with a myriad of stressors and challenges that can leave them feeling overwhelmed, anxious, and exhausted.

At the heart of this frustration and stress lies the relentless pursuit of perfection and success that permeates every aspect of girls' lives. From a young age, girls are taught to strive for excellence in all areas, from academics and extracurricular activities to personal appearance and social relationships. The pressure to excel in school, meet familial expectations, and conform to societal norms can create a relentless cycle of stress and anxiety that takes a toll on girls' mental and emotional well-being.

Moreover, girls may also face unique challenges and stressors that contribute to their feelings of frustration and overwhelm. From the complexities of navigating social dynamics and peer relationships to the demands of balancing multiple responsibilities and commitments, girls must juggle a multitude of demands and expectations that can leave them feeling stretched thin and unable to cope.

Furthermore, girls may also experience frustration and stress as they grapple with questions of identity, purpose, and belonging. In a world that often dictates narrow definitions of success and worth, girls may struggle to find their place and assert their identities in a society that values conformity and uniformity. The pressure to fit in, meet others' expectations, and live up to societal standards can create a profound sense of dissonance and alienation that fuels feelings of frustration and isolation.

In addition to these internal struggles, girls may also face external barriers to managing their stress and seeking support for their emotional well-being. Stigma surrounding mental health issues, lack of access to resources and support services, and cultural taboos around seeking help can all contribute to girls' reluctance to reach out for assistance when they need it most. As a result, many girls suffer in silence, grappling with their stress and anxiety alone and without the support they need to heal and thrive.

Despite these challenges, there are strategies and interventions that can help girls cope with frustration and stress and build resilience in the face of adversity. By practicing self-care, seeking support from trusted friends and adults, and developing healthy coping mechanisms, girls can learn to manage their stress and navigate life's challenges with grace and resilience. Through education, advocacy, and community outreach, we can ensure that every girl has the opportunity to access the care and support she needs to prioritize her mental and emotional well-being.

Part 3: Mental Health Resources

In the labyrinth of emotional turmoil, accessing mental health resources can serve as a lifeline for girls grappling with the complexities of adolescence and womanhood. Yet, for many, the journey to seek help and support can be fraught with obstacles and challenges that hinder their ability to access the care they need to thrive.

One of the primary barriers to accessing mental health resources is the pervasive stigma surrounding mental illness and seeking help for emotional struggles. In many communities, mental health issues are still viewed as a sign of weakness or moral failing, leading to shame and reluctance to seek assistance. This stigma can prevent girls from reaching out for help, fearing judgment or rejection from their peers, family, and community.

Moreover, even when girls are willing to seek help, they may encounter barriers such as lack of access to affordable and culturally competent care. Many communities lack adequate mental health resources, including trained professionals, support groups, and counseling services, leaving girls with few options for support. Additionally, the cost of mental health care can be prohibitive for many families, further limiting girls' ability to access the care they need.

Furthermore, cultural taboos and norms around mental health and help-seeking behaviors can also pose significant barriers to accessing care. In some cultures, mental illness is seen as a sign of spiritual or moral weakness, leading to reluctance to acknowledge or address mental health issues. Similarly, gender norms and expectations may dictate that girls should be strong and resilient, leading to pressure to conceal their struggles and suffer in silence.

Despite these challenges, there is hope for girls seeking support for their mental health and well-being. Increasing awareness and education about mental health issues, reducing stigma, and promoting open and honest conversations about emotions and mental health can help break down barriers to seeking help. Additionally, investing in culturally competent and affordable mental health services, including counseling, therapy, and support groups, can ensure that girls have access to the care they need to thrive.

Moreover, building supportive and inclusive communities that prioritize mental health and well-being can create a culture of acceptance and support where girls feel safe and empowered to seek help when they need it. By providing girls with the tools, resources, and support they need to prioritize their mental health, we can help them navigate life's challenges with resilience and strength.

In conclusion, accessing mental health resources is essential for promoting the well-being and resilience of girls as they navigate the complexities of adolescence and womanhood. By addressing stigma, increasing access to care, and building supportive communities, we can ensure that every girl has the opportunity to access the care and support she needs to thrive emotionally and mentally.

Part 4: Acceptance and Understanding

In the tumultuous landscape of emotional turmoil, acceptance and understanding serve as beacons of light, guiding girls through the darkest of storms and providing solace in times of uncertainty. Yet, for many, the journey to self-acceptance and understanding is fraught with obstacles and challenges that test the limits of their resilience and courage.

At the heart of acceptance lies the recognition that emotional struggles are a natural and inevitable part of the human experience, deserving of compassion and empathy rather than judgment or condemnation. By acknowledging the validity of their emotions and experiences, girls can begin to cultivate a sense of self-acceptance and understanding that allows them to embrace their strengths and vulnerabilities with grace and humility.

Moreover, acceptance is not just about recognizing one's own struggles, but also about extending compassion and understanding to others who may be facing similar challenges. By fostering a culture of empathy and solidarity, girls can create a supportive community where they feel seen, heard, and valued for who they are, free from the burden of shame or stigma.

In addition to acceptance, understanding plays a crucial role in girls' journey toward emotional well-being and resilience. By gaining insight into the root causes of their emotions and behaviors, girls can develop a deeper understanding of themselves and their experiences, empowering them to make informed decisions and take positive steps toward healing and growth.

Furthermore, understanding also involves recognizing the impact of external factors and societal influences on girls' emotional well-being. From systemic inequalities and social injustices to cultural norms and gender expectations, girls are often confronted with a myriad of external pressures and stressors that shape their emotional experiences and perceptions of themselves. By acknowledging these influences and challenging harmful norms and stereotypes, girls can begin to reclaim their autonomy and assert their right to emotional well-being and self-determination.

Despite the challenges and obstacles they may face, there is hope for girls seeking acceptance and understanding in their journey toward emotional well-being. By fostering a culture of acceptance, empathy, and understanding, we can create a world where every girl feels seen, heard, and valued for who she is, free from the burden of shame or stigma. Through education, advocacy, and community support, we can empower girls to embrace their emotions, cultivate resilience, and navigate life's challenges with courage and grace.

Chapter 5: Relationships and Compromises

Part 1: Family Relationships

In the intricate web of human connections, family relationships serve as the foundation upon which individuals build their identities, values, and sense of belonging. For girls, in particular, the dynamics of family relationships play a crucial role in shaping their self-esteem, aspirations, and emotional well-being. However, these relationships are often fraught with complexities and challenges that can impact girls' sense of self-worth and agency.

At the heart of family relationships lie expectations, traditions, and cultural norms that shape the roles and responsibilities assigned to girls within the family unit. From a young age, girls are socialized to fulfill certain roles and expectations based on their gender, often being assigned caretaking and domestic responsibilities that can limit their autonomy and opportunities for personal growth.

Moreover, family relationships can also be marked by power dynamics and hierarchies that influence girls' sense of agency and decision-making autonomy. In many households, patriarchal structures prevail, with male authority figures wielding disproportionate power and influence over family decisions and dynamics. This imbalance of power can leave girls feeling marginalized and disempowered, with limited say in matters that impact their lives and futures.

Furthermore, family relationships can also be sources of both support and conflict for girls as they navigate the complexities of adolescence and womanhood. While some families provide a nurturing and supportive environment that encourages girls to pursue their dreams and aspirations, others may impose strict rules and expectations that limit girls' autonomy and opportunities for growth.

Additionally, cultural and generational differences within families can also contribute to tensions and conflicts that impact girls' emotional well-being and sense of belonging. As girls navigate the delicate balance between honoring tradition and asserting their own values and beliefs, they may encounter resistance and pushback from family members who adhere to more traditional norms and expectations.

Despite these challenges, family relationships also offer opportunities for growth, resilience, and connection for girls as they navigate the complexities of adolescence and womanhood. By fostering open and honest communication, mutual respect, and empathy within the family unit, girls can cultivate supportive and nurturing relationships that empower them to assert their identities, pursue their passions, and navigate life's challenges with confidence and resilience.

Moreover, by challenging gender norms and stereotypes within the family unit, girls can help create a more inclusive and equitable environment where all members are valued and respected for their unique contributions and experiences. Through dialogue, education, and advocacy, families can become agents of change, promoting gender equality and empowerment for girls within their own homes and communities.

In conclusion, family relationships play a pivotal role in shaping girls' identities, values, and aspirations. By fostering supportive and nurturing environments within the family unit, girls can cultivate the resilience, confidence, and agency they need to navigate the complexities of adolescence and womanhood with grace and resilience. Through open communication, mutual respect, and empathy, families can become powerful allies in the journey toward gender equality and empowerment for girls everywhere.

Part 2: Romantic Relationships

In the intricate dance of love and companionship, romantic relationships hold a special place in the lives of girls, offering the promise of intimacy, connection, and companionship. However, navigating the complexities of romantic relationships can be both exhilarating and challenging for girls as they navigate the landscape of love, desire, and commitment.

At the heart of romantic relationships lie notions of love, attraction, and compatibility that shape girls' perceptions of themselves and their worth. From a young age, girls are bombarded with messages and images that romanticize love and idealize relationships, leading them to internalize unrealistic expectations and standards for romantic partners and relationships.

Moreover, romantic relationships can also be sites of power dynamics and inequality that impact girls' sense of agency and autonomy. In many heterosexual relationships, gender norms and stereotypes dictate that boys should take the lead and girls should be passive and accommodating, leading to imbalances of power and influence that can undermine girls' confidence and self-worth.

Furthermore, romantic relationships can also be sources of both joy and pain for girls as they navigate the highs and lows of love and heartbreak. While healthy relationships can offer support, validation, and companionship, unhealthy relationships marked by control, manipulation, and abuse can erode girls' self-esteem and well-being, leaving them feeling isolated and powerless.

Additionally, societal expectations and pressures surrounding romantic relationships can also impact girls' experiences and perceptions of love and intimacy. From cultural norms and religious beliefs to media portrayals and peer influences, girls are bombarded with messages that dictate how they should look, act, and behave in romantic relationships, leading to feelings of insecurity and inadequacy if they do not measure up to these unrealistic standards.

Despite these challenges, romantic relationships also offer opportunities for growth, self-discovery, and personal development for girls as they navigate the complexities of love and companionship. By fostering open and honest communication, mutual respect, and trust within romantic partnerships, girls can cultivate healthy and fulfilling relationships that empower them to assert their needs, boundaries, and desires with confidence and agency.

Moreover, by challenging traditional gender roles and expectations within romantic relationships, girls can help create more equitable and inclusive partnerships where both partners are valued and respected for their unique strengths and contributions. Through dialogue, education, and advocacy, girls can become agents of change, promoting gender equality and empowerment within their own relationships and communities.

In conclusion, romantic relationships play a significant role in shaping girls' perceptions of love, intimacy, and self-worth. By fostering healthy and equitable partnerships, girls can cultivate the resilience, confidence, and agency they need to navigate the complexities of romantic love with grace and resilience. Through open communication, mutual respect, and trust, girls can create relationships that honor their individuality and empower them to pursue love and companionship on their own terms.

Part 3: Matrimonial Expectations

In the intricate tapestry of societal expectations and familial traditions, matrimonial expectations weigh heavily on the shoulders of girls as they navigate the journey toward adulthood and independence. From a young age, girls are socialized to aspire to marriage as a marker of success and fulfillment, with societal norms and cultural expectations dictating that marriage is the ultimate goal for women.

At the heart of matrimonial expectations lie notions of duty, obligation, and conformity that shape girls' perceptions of their roles and responsibilities within the family unit. From a young age, girls are taught to prioritize the needs and desires of others above their own, with marriage often seen as a means of securing financial stability, social status, and familial approval.

Moreover, matrimonial expectations can also be sources of pressure and anxiety for girls as they navigate the complexities of courtship, engagement, and marriage. In many cultures, arranged marriages are still common, with girls expected to acquiesce to the wishes of their families and conform to cultural and religious traditions that dictate who they should marry and when.

Furthermore, matrimonial expectations can also perpetuate harmful gender stereotypes and inequalities that limit girls' autonomy and opportunities for personal growth and fulfillment. In many societies, girls are expected to prioritize their roles as wives and mothers above all else, with little regard for their own ambitions, dreams, and aspirations outside of the home.

Additionally, matrimonial expectations can also impact girls' perceptions of their worth and value as individuals, with marriage often seen as a measure of their desirability and worthiness as potential partners. From a young age, girls are taught to equate their worth with their ability to attract a suitable partner and fulfill the expectations of their families and communities, leading to feelings of inadequacy and insecurity if they do not meet these standards.

Despite these challenges, matrimonial expectations also offer opportunities for girls to assert their autonomy, agency, and self-determination as they navigate the complexities of courtship and marriage. By challenging traditional gender roles and expectations, girls can carve out paths for themselves that honor their individuality and aspirations, rather than conforming to societal norms and expectations.

Moreover, by advocating for gender equality and empowerment within their own families and communities, girls can help create a more inclusive and equitable society where all individuals have the freedom and opportunity to pursue their own paths to happiness and fulfillment. Through dialogue, education, and advocacy, girls can become agents of change, challenging harmful norms and stereotypes that perpetuate inequality and injustice within the institution of marriage.

In conclusion, matrimonial expectations play a significant role in shaping girls' perceptions of their roles and responsibilities within the family unit. By challenging traditional norms and expectations, girls can assert their autonomy and agency, and create paths for themselves that honor their individuality and aspirations. Through dialogue, education, and advocacy, girls can help create a more inclusive and equitable society where all individuals have the freedom and opportunity to pursue their own paths to happiness and fulfillment.

Part 4: Self-Respect and Autonomy

In the intricate dance of relationships, self-respect and autonomy stand as pillars of strength and empowerment for girls as they navigate the complexities of interpersonal connections and societal expectations. Central to the notion of self-respect is the recognition of one's inherent worth and dignity, irrespective of external validation or approval. Similarly, autonomy refers to the ability to make independent choices and decisions that align with one's values, goals, and aspirations.

At the heart of self-respect and autonomy lie the principles of agency, empowerment, and self-assertion that empower girls to assert their boundaries, advocate for their needs, and prioritize their well-being in relationships. From a young age, girls are taught to value themselves and their unique qualities, cultivating a sense of self-worth that serves as a shield against external pressures and expectations.

Moreover, self-respect and autonomy also involve the recognition of one's rights and responsibilities within relationships, including the right to set boundaries, express needs, and assert preferences without fear of judgment or reprisal. By honoring their own boundaries and respecting those of others, girls can create healthy and equitable relationships built on mutual trust, respect, and understanding.

Furthermore, self-respect and autonomy enable girls to navigate the complexities of romantic relationships with confidence and integrity, refusing to compromise their values or sacrifice their autonomy for the sake of companionship or approval. By prioritizing their own well-being and happiness, girls can cultivate relationships that honor their individuality and empower them to pursue love and companionship on their own terms.

Additionally, self-respect and autonomy also play a crucial role in girls' ability to resist external pressures and expectations related to marriage and family life. By asserting their right to make independent choices and decisions about their futures, girls can challenge traditional norms and expectations that limit their autonomy and opportunities for personal growth and fulfillment.

Despite the challenges and obstacles they may face, self-respect and autonomy offer girls a path to empowerment and liberation from the constraints of societal expectations and gender norms. By embracing their inherent worth and asserting their autonomy in relationships and life choices, girls can carve out paths for themselves that honor their individuality, aspirations, and dreams.

Moreover, by advocating for gender equality and empowerment within their own relationships and communities, girls can help create a more inclusive and equitable society where all individuals have the freedom and opportunity to pursue their own paths to happiness and fulfillment. Through dialogue, education, and advocacy, girls can become agents of change, challenging harmful norms and stereotypes that perpetuate inequality and injustice within relationships and society at large.

In conclusion, self-respect and autonomy serve as guiding principles for girls as they navigate the complexities of relationships, marriage, and societal expectations. By honoring their own worth and asserting their autonomy, girls can create paths for themselves that honor their individuality and empower them to pursue happiness and fulfillment on their own terms. Through dialogue, education, and advocacy, girls can help create a world where all individuals have the freedom and opportunity to live authentically and pursue their dreams with courage and conviction.

Chapter 6: Towards Empowerment

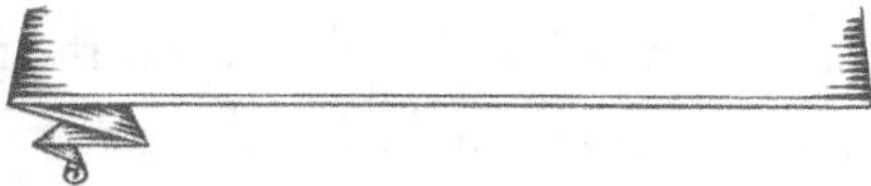

Part 1: Breaking Barriers

In the journey towards empowerment, breaking barriers stands as a pivotal moment for girls as they challenge the constraints of societal norms and expectations, paving the way for greater freedom, equality, and opportunity. At the heart of this quest lies the courage and resilience of girls who dare to defy the status quo and forge paths of their own, despite the obstacles and challenges they may face.

Breaking barriers encompasses a multitude of experiences and achievements, from shattering glass ceilings in traditionally male-dominated fields to challenging cultural taboos and stereotypes that limit girls' potential and aspirations. Whether it's excelling in academics, pursuing careers in STEM fields, or advocating for social justice and equality, girls around the world are making their mark and inspiring others to follow in their footsteps.

Moreover, breaking barriers also involves dismantling systemic inequalities and injustices that perpetuate gender discrimination and oppression, creating a more inclusive and equitable society where all individuals have the opportunity to thrive. From advocating for equal pay and access to education to challenging discriminatory laws and practices, girls are leading the charge for change and driving progress towards gender equality and empowerment.

Furthermore, breaking barriers is not just about individual achievements, but also about collective action and solidarity among girls and women who stand together in solidarity to challenge injustice and create a better world for future generations. By amplifying their voices, advocating for their rights, and supporting one another in their quest for equality, girls are building a powerful movement that is transforming societies and rewriting the narrative of what is possible for girls and women everywhere.

Additionally, breaking barriers involves challenging internalized beliefs and stereotypes that hold girls back from realizing their full potential and asserting their autonomy and agency. By cultivating self-confidence, resilience, and a sense of purpose, girls can overcome self-doubt and fear, and embrace their power to effect change in their own lives and communities.

Despite the challenges and obstacles they may face, girls are breaking barriers and defying expectations in every corner of the globe, proving that with courage, determination, and solidarity, anything is possible. As they continue to push boundaries and challenge the status quo, girls are paving the way for a more inclusive, equitable, and just world where all individuals have the opportunity to thrive and fulfill their dreams. Through their actions and advocacy, girls are not only changing their own lives but also shaping the future for generations to come.

In conclusion, breaking barriers is a powerful act of defiance and liberation for girls as they challenge the constraints of gender inequality and oppression, paving the way for greater freedom, equality, and opportunity. By daring to dream big, stand tall, and demand change, girls are reshaping the world and creating a future where all individuals have the opportunity to thrive and fulfill their potential, regardless of gender or background.

Part 2: Empowerment Tools

In the journey towards empowerment, girls wield a diverse array of tools and resources that serve as catalysts for change, enabling them to overcome barriers, assert their rights, and pursue their dreams with courage and conviction. From education and skill development to advocacy and mentorship, these empowerment tools equip girls with the knowledge, skills, and support they need to navigate the complexities of adolescence and womanhood with resilience and confidence.

At the heart of empowerment tools lies education, which serves as a cornerstone for girls' personal and professional development, providing them with the knowledge, skills, and opportunities they need to succeed in life. By investing in girls' education, communities can break the cycle of poverty, improve health outcomes, and foster economic growth and prosperity for all.

Moreover, empowerment tools also encompass skill development programs and initiatives that equip girls with the practical skills and competencies they need to thrive in a rapidly changing world. From vocational training programs to entrepreneurship workshops, these initiatives empower girls to unlock their potential, pursue their passions, and create pathways to economic independence and self-sufficiency.

Furthermore, empowerment tools include access to information and resources that enable girls to make informed decisions about their health, rights, and futures. By providing girls with access to sexual and reproductive health services, information about their rights, and opportunities for civic engagement and leadership, communities can empower girls to take control of their lives and advocate for change in their communities.

Additionally, mentorship and support networks play a crucial role in empowering girls to overcome obstacles, navigate challenges, and realize their full potential. By connecting girls with mentors and role models who can offer guidance, support, and encouragement, communities can help girls build confidence, resilience, and a sense of belonging that empowers them to pursue their dreams with determination and courage.

Despite the challenges and obstacles they may face, girls are harnessing the power of empowerment tools to create positive change in their lives and communities. By investing in education, skill development, access to information, and mentorship, communities can unlock the potential of girls and unleash a wave of progress and prosperity that benefits everyone.

In conclusion, empowerment tools are essential resources that enable girls to overcome barriers, assert their rights, and pursue their dreams with courage and conviction. By investing in education, skill development, access to information, and mentorship, communities can empower girls to create brighter futures for themselves and build a more inclusive, equitable, and just world for all.

Part 3: Future Aspirations

In the journey towards empowerment, girls envision a future filled with possibilities, where they are free to pursue their passions, fulfill their potential, and contribute meaningfully to society. Central to this vision are the aspirations and dreams of girls who dare to imagine a world where gender equality is not just a distant ideal, but a lived reality for all.

At the heart of future aspirations lies the belief in the power of education to unlock doors of opportunity and possibility for girls, providing them with the knowledge, skills, and confidence they need to pursue their dreams and aspirations. By investing in education, communities can empower girls to break free from the constraints of poverty and discrimination, and build brighter futures for themselves and their communities.

Moreover, future aspirations encompass a wide range of goals and ambitions, from pursuing careers in STEM fields to becoming leaders in their communities and advocates for social change. By supporting girls' aspirations and providing them with opportunities to explore their interests and talents, communities can help girls realize their full potential and become agents of change in their own lives and communities.

Furthermore, future aspirations involve challenging traditional gender roles and expectations that limit girls' opportunities and constrain their potential. By breaking free from stereotypes and societal norms, girls can assert their right to choose their own paths and pursue their passions without fear of judgment or discrimination.

Additionally, future aspirations involve creating supportive environments and opportunities for girls to thrive, including access to mentorship, role models, and networks that can help them navigate the challenges and obstacles they may face along the way. By connecting girls with mentors and allies who can offer guidance, support, and encouragement, communities can empower girls to overcome barriers and realize their dreams with confidence and resilience.

Despite the challenges and obstacles they may face, girls are forging ahead with courage and determination, driven by their aspirations for a better future for themselves and future generations. By investing in girls' education, supporting their aspirations, and creating opportunities for them to succeed, communities can unlock the potential of girls and build a brighter, more inclusive, and equitable future for all.

In conclusion, future aspirations are a driving force for girls as they journey towards empowerment, inspiring them to dream big, aim high, and work tirelessly to create a better world for themselves and future generations. By investing in education, supporting their ambitions, and creating opportunities for them to succeed, communities can empower girls to realize their full potential and build a future where all individuals have the opportunity to thrive and fulfill their dreams.

Part 4: Realistic Touch

In the pursuit of empowerment, it's essential to ground aspirations in practicality and realism, acknowledging the challenges and obstacles that may arise along the way while maintaining a steadfast commitment to progress and change. This realistic touch serves as a compass, guiding girls through the complexities of their journey and empowering them to navigate obstacles with resilience and determination.

At the heart of this realistic touch lies the recognition of the systemic barriers and inequalities that continue to impede girls' progress and limit their opportunities for advancement. From entrenched gender norms and stereotypes to economic disparities and social injustices, girls face a myriad of obstacles that can hinder their path to empowerment and success.

Moreover, a realistic touch involves understanding the importance of incremental progress and small victories along the way, recognizing that meaningful change often takes time and persistence. By celebrating achievements, no matter how small, and learning from setbacks and failures, girls can build resilience and determination that will sustain them on their journey towards empowerment.

Furthermore, a realistic touch involves recognizing the importance of self-care and well-being in the pursuit of empowerment, acknowledging that girls cannot pour from an empty cup. By prioritizing their physical, mental, and emotional health, girls can ensure they have the strength and resilience to overcome challenges and continue moving forward on their path to empowerment.

Additionally, a realistic touch involves fostering a sense of community and solidarity among girls, recognizing that they are not alone in their journey and that together, they are stronger. By building networks of support and allyship, girls can amplify their voices, advocate for change, and create a more inclusive and equitable world for all.

Despite the challenges and obstacles they may face, a realistic touch reminds girls that progress is possible, even in the face of adversity. By staying grounded in reality, acknowledging the complexities of their journey, and maintaining a steadfast commitment to their goals and aspirations, girls can overcome obstacles, defy expectations, and create a brighter future for themselves and future generations.

In conclusion, a realistic touch is essential in the pursuit of empowerment, guiding girls through the complexities of their journey and empowering them to navigate obstacles with resilience and determination. By acknowledging challenges, celebrating achievements, and prioritizing well-being, girls can build the strength and resilience they need to create meaningful change in their lives and communities.

Conclusion

IN THE PAGES OF "HIDDEN Struggles; The Unseen Challenges Of Women," we have delved into the intricate tapestry of girls' lives, exploring the myriad challenges and obstacles they face on their journey towards empowerment. From societal constraints and familial expectations to self-esteem struggles and relationship dynamics, the journey of girls is marked by complexities, resilience, and the relentless pursuit of freedom, equality, and opportunity.

Throughout this exploration, we have witnessed the transformative power of empowerment, as girls defy expectations, challenge norms, and assert their rights with courage and conviction. From breaking barriers in traditionally male-dominated fields to advocating for social change and gender equality, girls around the world are rewriting the narrative of what is possible, paving the way for a more inclusive, equitable, and just society for all.

At the heart of this journey towards empowerment lies the recognition of the inherent worth and dignity of every girl, irrespective of her background, circumstances, or aspirations. By honoring their voices, valuing their contributions, and supporting their dreams, we can create a world where all girls have the opportunity to thrive, fulfill their potential, and lead lives of meaning and purpose.

As we reflect on the stories, insights, and experiences shared within these pages, let us remember that the journey towards empowerment is ongoing, requiring sustained effort, commitment, and solidarity from individuals, communities, and societies alike. By standing together in solidarity, advocating for change, and creating opportunities for all girls to succeed, we can build a future where every girl has the freedom, opportunity, and support she needs to live a life of dignity, equality, and empowerment.

In closing, let us embrace the call to action that echoes through the pages of this book, committing ourselves to the cause of empowerment and justice for all girls, everywhere. For in their journey lies the promise of a brighter, more inclusive, and equitable world for generations to come.

About the Author

Mrigendra Bharti, born on June 29, 2004, in South Delhi, India, is a multifaceted individual recognized as the owner of Mrigendra Bharti Group InfoTech India Co. Pvt Ltd. Beyond his entrepreneurial endeavors, he is a distinguished music producer, director, and a budding writer.

Embarking on his professional journey at a young age, Mrigendra Bharti's visionary leadership has led to the establishment of several successful ventures, including Croma Music Series Entertainment, Sellbrochure, Fauget Innovative, and more.

What sets Mrigendra apart is his early initiation into the world of business. His foray into the unknown realms of entrepreneurship began during his 10th-grade years, where he delved into the music industry. This initial venture laid the foundation for subsequent achievements, showcasing his dedication and resilience.

Having honed his skills in music, Mrigendra Bharti not only demonstrated significant growth in his craft but also expanded his professional network. His passion extends beyond music, encompassing app and website development, as well as graphic design.

Fueled by his creative aspirations, Mrigendra established the Mrigendra Bharti Group, a company specializing in website and app development. Currently, he collaborates with a dedicated team, collectively working on ambitious projects that promise innovation and excellence.

Mrigendra's journey serves as an inspiration, particularly for today's students, highlighting the potential of youthful determination and the ability to transform innovative ideas into successful businesses. As he continues to make strides in various domains, Mrigendra Bharti remains a dynamic force, contributing vibrancy to the realms of business, music, and technology.

Read more at https://www.imwriter-mrigendra.rf.gd.